THERE'S ONLY ONE
DANNY OGLE

Helena Pielichaty

ILLUSTRATED BY
GLYN GOODWIN

OXFORD
UNIVERSITY PRESS

ACKNOWLEDGEMENTS

for Pete, Jurek, Vytas, Big Dave and all who sit in the John Smith Stand,
as well as to Nick and Aaron in the posh end, for their timeless
comments on the beautiful game.
I would also like to thank Steve Lee and John Wolfenden for helping
me in my research about youth teams and junior football

This book is dedicated to David Moulds, even if he does support Leicester
City, for his support and encouragement

OXFORD
UNIVERSITY PRESS

Great Clarendon Street, Oxford OX2 6DP

Oxford University Press is a department of the University of Oxford.
It furthers the University's objective of excellence in research, scholarship,
and education by publishing worldwide in

Oxford New York

Auckland Cape Town Dar es Salaam Hong Kong Karachi
Kuala Lumpur Madrid Melbourne Mexico City Nairobi
New Delhi Shanghai Taipei Toronto

With offices in

Argentina Austria Brazil Chile Czech Republic France Greece
Guatemala Hungary Italy Japan Poland Portugal Singapore
South Korea Switzerland Thailand Turkey Ukraine Vietnam

Oxford is a registered trade mark of Oxford University Press
in the UK and in certain other countries

British Library Cataloguing in Publication Data available

ISBN-13: 978-0-19-275235-2
ISBN-10: 0-19-275235-9

7 9 10 8 6

Printed in Great Britain by
Cox & Wyman Ltd, Reading, Berks

THERE'S ONLY ONE
DANNY OGLE

When Danny moves to the countryside the only
good thing to come out of it is that he mi⸱ ⸱ have
a chance at getting picked for the school ⸱⸱⸱⸱
team. Danny loves football. He eats, breathes ⸱
sleeps football. But will the other kids ⸱
school want to be friends with him? And, ⸱
want him in their team?

Helena Pielichaty ⸱⸱⸱ born in Sweden to an Eng⸱ ⸱⸱⸱other
and Polish-Russian father. Her family moved to ⸱⸱⸱kshire
when Helena was five where she lived until qualifying as a
teacher from Bretton Hall College in 1978. She has taught in
various parts of the country including East Grinstead, Oxford,
and Sheffield. Helena now lives with her husband in
Nottinghamshire where she divides her time between looking
after their two children, writing, and following the trials and
tribulations of Huddersfield Town A.F.C. *There's Only One
Danny Ogle* is her sixth novel for Oxford University Press.

1

Hi, my name is Danny Ogle and my life is over. Want to know why? We've moved to the countryside. Any old mates who want to find me can contact me at:

Danny Ogle
   Dump Cottage
      Dead Boring Lane
         Little to Do
            Middle of Nowhere
               England

No offence if you like living in a village. Cows and fields and fresh air are fine if you like that kind of thing but I'm a town boy. I was born in a town, grew up in a town, and support a football team with 'town' in its name.

A few months ago, when Mum said we were moving somewhere better, what I thought she meant was:

◉ My bedroom window would overlook the McAlpine Stadium
◉ We'd have Sky TV
◉ The garden would be big enough for five-a-side matches
◉ McDonald's would be across the road
◉ I wouldn't have to change schools so I could try out for the A team.

What she really meant was:

◉ My bedroom window overlooked miles and miles of *nothing*
◉ We'd have ordinary TV but sky was available if I looked outside (ha ha)

◎The garden was big enough for a football pitch but I'd have to get rid of the orchard first

◎Forget McDonald's. All we had was one piddly shop run by someone called Mrs Dobb

◎But worst of all, not only did I have to change schools, I had to change counties.

Like I said, my life is over.

2

It was Gran who helped me to see things differently. Gran's an auxiliary nurse at the hospital. She once did our ace defender Kevin Green's bedpans when he had a broken leg; she's *that* famous.

Last night we had our usual conversation. It went something like this:

On the Phone

Gran: Hello, love. Have you finished unpacking yet?

Me: Sort of.

Gran: Your mum says the cottage is lovely.

Me: It's all right.

Gran: It's a pity you're only renting it. Where is it the owners live? Dubai?

Me: Something like that.

Gran: Hey! You start your new school next week, don't you? What's it called again?

Me: (dead grumpy) Westhorpe Primary School for Turnips.

Gran: (sighs patiently) Come on, Danny, change the record. Think positive.

Me: How can I? I won't know one person there except Karla and sisters don't count. I hate change.

Gran: I thought you wanted to be a professional footballer when you grow up?

Me: I do!

Gran: Well, what about when you're transferred? You'll need to move from one end of the country to the other every few seasons then.

Me: I guess.

Gran: Have you found out about Westhorpe's football team yet?

Me: No.

Gran: Your mum was telling me there's under thirty pupils. I bet you get straight into the 'A' team—they might even make you captain, a lad with your talent and experience.

Now that gave me something to think about. No matter how much I tried at my old school the coach always stuck me in the 'B' squad. It wasn't because I wasn't good enough for the 'A' lot, you understand, it was just that we were an outstanding year with hundreds to choose from. Plus coach wanted someone decent in the 'B's so they wouldn't lose heart. I was sacrificed, actually.

Inspired, I handed over the phone to Mum and dashed outside to practise my ball juggling. There was no point allowing my skills to erode. A captain has to set a good example.

3

As soon as Mum had finished on the phone I asked her where the school handbook was. 'The one you said you'd rather support United than read?' she teased.

'That's the one.'

'Next to the microwave.'

'Thanks, chuck,' I said, jogging into the kitchen.

She followed me, grinning, obviously delighted to have her old son back again. 'Looking for something in particular?' she asked.

'Team details,' I replied, flicking through the pages. 'School uniform—not interested—school dinners—no way—school rules—not bothered—job vacancies—who cares? I can't find anything about the football teams,' I said in disgust. 'At Frank Worthington's there were tons.'

'Let me have a look,' Mum said. 'Hmm . . . could this be it?' She pointed a fingernail at something called 'After School Activities'.

Together we scanned the columns.

Westhorpe School After School Activities

3.30 p.m. to 5.00 p.m. daily. Come to as many as you like. Tuck shop every day.

Choose from:

Mondays	Chess Club
Tuesdays	Country Dancing
Wednesdays	Gardening Club
Thursdays	Computer Club
Fridays	Westhorpe Wanderers

'Do you think that's the name of the football team?' I asked doubtfully, staring at Friday.

'The Westhorpe Wanderers? Like Bolton Wanderers? Could be,' Mum agreed.

'It's got to be, hasn't it? There's nothing else near. I wonder who takes it? There's no names.'

'You'll find out soon enough. Have you seen this?'

'What?'

Mum turned over to the last page in the handbook. The page was blank apart from a heading inviting new pupils to write about themselves. She had mentioned it a dozen times before but I'd 'forgotten' about it. I hated writing—especially about myself. 'Do I have to?' I whinged.

'It's up to you,' she shrugged, 'but why miss a chance to impress them? If nothing comes on the market we're going to be here until Christmas at least—that must be enough time for a few matches. You could make out you're on the transfer list and they're lucky to have you.'

'They are lucky to have me!' I agreed. 'Got a pen?'

4

Mrs Bulinski, my new Head as well as class teacher, was a stocky woman with dark hair and square red glasses. Karla, who was going through a reading-nothing-but-Roald Dahl phase, stared at her and whispered nervously, 'She looks like *Miss Trunchbull*.'

I was thinking the same thing but I was too busy trying to look keen and captain-ish to whisper back. The Head beamed at us both before addressing the school and suddenly she didn't look like Miss Trunchbull at all—she looked kind and friendly. 'Well, everybody, welcome back to a new year at Westhorpe. Did you all have a good holiday?' There was much nodding and 'yer-ing' from the kids around me on the carpet. They seemed cool enough. One boy, a kid called Curtis, had already said I could join his mates at break. I began to relax.

Mrs Bulinski beamed again. 'Good. Firstly, let me introduce you to Mrs Speed. Mrs Speed is on supply until we get a new teacher.' Eyes turned to the side of the classroom where a tall, spindly woman with grey hair nodded and smiled from behind the piano. I tried to guess which one coached The Wanderers. Neither looked exactly sporty but that meant nothing. There had been a dead fat kid called Martin Mallinson at my old school who could outrun the lot of us.

Mrs Bulinski switched her attention to Karla and me. 'And we're very pleased to have two new pupils starting today as well; Danny, a Year Five and Karla, a Year Three.'

I felt everyone staring at me so I focused on

my new trainers. 'Would one of you like to tell us a bit about yourselves?'

Karla shook her head, even though I knew she had spent ages on her introduction. Realizing she was even more nervous than I was, I gave her a 'don't worry' dig and stood up. Pulling the sheet from out of my pocket, I cleared my throat, and began to read:

A little bit about me
(for new pupils only)

Hi, my name is Danny Ogle and I'm nine and a half—I'll be ten in February. I live with my mum, Debbie, her partner Steve, and my sister, Karla. Steve is a photographer and Mum is a nursery nurse. My dad lives in Germany. I don't see him much. I'll let Karla tell you about herself.

I'm the odd one out in my family because I'm football mad. The only other

---

person who likes it is my gran, though my grandad did, too, when he was alive. My gran takes me to see all Town's home matches when she can. Town's the name of the team I support. I've supported them since I was 6. I have two dreams: one is to be chosen as a mascot and run on the pitch at the McAlpine Stadium. The second is to be selected for Town's Centre of Excellence. Kevin Green is my favourite player because he's hard and gets stuck in.

I love playing football, as well as watching it. I like mid-field or attack but I'm very versatile. My coach said I was good at finding space and ball control. Most important is that I am not a ball-hog or a goal-hanger.

I am never late for practices and am available for any home or away fixtures. I

don't mind taking the kit home to wash
but we only have one car and Steve uses
that a lot for his work so I might need a
lift to away games. I look forward to
joining the Westhorpe Wanderers and
promise to help bring back a trophy or
two this season.

Someone laughed just then and put me off.
Mrs Bulinski cleaned her glasses with the edge
of her skirt and gave the culprit a deadeye at
the same time. 'That was very good, Danny,
well done, but I think you've got hold of the
wrong end of the stick. Spencer Mason, as you
found Dan's mistake so amusing perhaps you'll
have the good manners to explain to him what
the Westhorpe Wanderers do.'

This Spencer kid stared dumbly into space.
'They wander around Westhorpe,' he said in a
bored voice.

'Wondering why they bother!' added a
comedian next to him.

Mrs Bulinski held up a warning finger and they shut up. 'The Westhorpe Wanderers go on walks and find out all sorts about nature, Danny. I'm afraid they've got nothing to do with football.'

'When's football practice then?' I asked.

'It isn't, I'm afraid. We don't have a team here.'

'You can always try country dancing!' the Spencer kid shouted out dead sarky.

'Lend me one of your skirts then!' I fired back. Loads of kids laughed but Spencer and his mate stared sourly into my face.

Great.

5

'Give this to *them* when we get in,' I ordered Karla at the end of school. I thrust a note into her hand and hurried along Low Street.

At home I ran upstairs before either Mum or Steve had a chance to start grilling me. I heard Mum ask Karla what the matter was but I banged the bedroom door shut before I could hear her reply.

A few minutes later Mum tapped on the door and entered. 'What's this mean?' she asked softly. She read out my note:

1. No I didn't
2. Sausage casserole, lumps of mash, iced bun
3. No one

I sighed heavily. 'It's the answer to the questions you always ask when I come in from school.'

'Ah. I see. So, one, you didn't have a nice day, two, you had sausage casserole for lunch and three, you sat by yourself.'

'That's about the size of it,' I mumbled.

'Karla told me about the football team.'

'Huh!'

'I'm sorry, Danny.'

I just stared at the wall. Mum and Steve didn't really understand about football so I couldn't tell her how I felt. How nothing gives me that tingly feeling in the pit of my stomach like when I'm running onto the pitch at the start of a match with the team, getting into position and waiting for the whistle to blow. And how nothing *in this universe* compares to scoring a goal. *Nothing*. Without any of that, school would be torture.

'It's early days yet, love,' Mum said, 'and if we don't find a house to buy that we like in Westhorpe we might look in one of the bigger villages and the first thing we'll check out is whether the school has a football team.'

'Promise?'

'Promise.'

I felt better already. My mum always keeps her promises.

Meanwhile, I took Gran's advice and made the most of things. I kept my head down and listened in class, answered a few questions now and again and even joined in with singing hymns during assembly. I had to wait until Friday last thing, though, for Games.

Mrs Bulinski emerged from the office in her ordinary clothes, the whistle dangling round her neck the only clue to what was next. I didn't care. At last we were going to have a decent lesson. I was ready in a flash and asked if I could help put out the equipment. 'Equipment? Oh, yes, maybe,' she said, peering through the window. 'I don't like the look of those clouds.'

'Here we go,' Curtis muttered.

I glanced out. There was one tiny cloud about seven hundred miles away. 'Oh, that's nothing,' I said, 'we used to play in hailstones in Yorkshire.'

Mrs Bulinski shuddered. 'Perish the thought,' she said and dispatched Curtis and me to the shed.

I waited impatiently for him to open the door. 'What are we getting out then?' I asked eagerly. 'Cones? Nets? How many balls do we need?'

'Whatever,' Curtis said, standing back to let me go in first.

It was the crummiest games cupboard I'd ever seen. Plastic hoops had been left scattered amongst tangled skipping ropes and soggy beanbags. A rusty netball post lay sideways across like a tree struck by lightning. Then, in a far corner, I saw it. I let out a low gasp of horror and stumbled forward.

'What's up?' Curtis asked in alarm. 'Have you found Mrs Dobb's missing cat? Is it dead? Don't show me if it is—I'll puke.'

'Worse. Look.'

I held out the sad leather ball cradled in my arms. It had been good quality once but was now dirty and deflated, its whole side caved in like a baseball glove. 'That's criminal, that is,' I said.

'Get used to it, mate,' Curtis replied, 'Mrs B hates PE.'

Before I had time to have a heart attack, Alfie Cruickshank, a Year Four, came belting round the corner. 'You've to come back in—we're doing mat work.'

'See what I mean?' Curtis shrugged, locking up again.

'You mean this is normal?'

He nodded. 'She does it every lesson. By the time we've got the mats out we'll have done three arms stretches and a forward roll and that'll be it. Like I said, get used to it.'

'Used to it? Used to no PE?'

'Yeah. We don't even bother bringing kit in any more, except for swimming on Wednesdays.'

My life was *so* over.

7

I couldn't wait to get home. I was going to pack straightaway then phone AA Roadwatch for the route back to Gran's. If Mum refused to take me I'd walk the whole one hundred and four miles. One thing was certain. There was *no way* I was staying at Westhorpe Primary.

That was until Mrs Bulinski dropped her bombshell just before half three. 'I've been mulling over Danny's speech yesterday,' she began, 'and it got me thinking. We have never been a very sporty school, but I do hate seeing enthusiasm like Danny's go to waste, and I know he's not the only one. Now, it's no secret that I don't know one end of a football court from another but if any Year Fours, Fives, or Sixes are interested I'm willing to organize some sort of football practice. *Is* anyone interested?'

My arm shot up faster than a rocket. Five or six others joined me. 'Oh,' Mrs B said, surprised. 'OK. Now keep your hand up if you know any grown-up who'd like to train you.' Every hand fell, including mine. I knew neither Mum nor Steve had time. 'Hmm, just as I thought. Never mind, I'll send a note home but if no one volunteers by the end of next week we'll have to think again. Meanwhile, I'll put a notice on the board for you to sign up. Fewer than ten and it won't be worth it,' she warned.

I belted home. 'Turkey dinosaurs, chips, and cornflake tart!' I gasped, adding quickly, 'Which one of you wants to coach football?'

'Football? What's that?' Mum teased, then said no, like I knew she would.

'Can't, Dan. I never know where I'll be one day from the next with work,' Steve said, like I knew he would.

It was the same with Curtis and Alfie when they called round. Alfie's parents both worked and Curtis's mum had just had a baby. 'Someone'll do it,' I said, trying to be optimistic.

'I want to know why Mrs B's suddenly starting a team. She's always said no before,' Curtis said.

Alfie answered: 'Oh, that's simple. Remember the Huckerby twins left to go to Tuxton because they wanted to do more sport?'

'Yeah.'

'My mum's a governor and I heard her telling Dad Mrs B's panicking in case Oggy goes, too. We've got an inspection next term and the school might close if we don't get numbers up.'

'Where's Tuxton?' I asked.

'It's another village school like ours except a bit bigger and they win loads of tournaments.'

'I wanna go to Tuxton!' I said, pretending to cry.

'No you don't. Their Head Mr Girton's really mean and strict. Mrs Bulinski's miles better.'

There was nothing wrong with 'strict' in my book, as long as people were fair with it. Still, you couldn't tell that to kids who weren't used to the sporting mentality so I just shrugged and led the way round the side of the house. 'Come on, let's have a kick about,' I said. I chalked the outline of a goal mouth against the gable end and we took turns, two on one, tackling and shooting.

Curtis had been to a football summer school over in Lincoln, so he was pretty good. He got

the ball off me nearly every time. 'I thought country kids couldn't play,' I grumbled.

'Think again, town boy!' he yelled, belting the ball against the brickwork.

Alfie had never played in his life and it showed. His toe-ender kicks were all over the place and he shouted 'Help me, Mummy!' as a joke if anyone tried to tackle him. Then he missed the ball completely and fell onto the road. We took him inside and Steve cleaned him up.

'We need a proper pitch to play on,' I said, 'why don't we go down to the school field?'

The school field was across a small side road opposite the school. It had full-sized goalposts but I hadn't been able to suss out the state of the grass because the field gate was always padlocked. Curtis told me why. 'It's out of bounds except during lessons; the caretaker has to protect his onions,' he explained.

'Do what?'

'Protect his onions. Mr Spanner grows vegetables round the edges of the field.'

'Never! How come?'

'I think the field used to be bigger and years ago Westhorpe pupils used to grow things on it but then they stopped and the council sold part of it for housing.'

'The Lawns Estate,' Alfie informed us

through clenched teeth, as Steve dabbed a little too hard.

Curtis nodded then continued. 'Mr Spanner had to move the vegetable patches closer and I think they've kind of accidentally-on-purpose spread since Mrs Bulinski came because she hardly uses it. He's got clematis growing up the goalposts if you look closely.'

'Now I've heard everything,' I said in amazement.

Alfie was picking shale out of his bony kneecap. 'We can practise in my garden until we find somewhere else,' he offered.

'Is it big enough?' I asked.

'Oh, I think you'll find it adequate.'

'Cool. How about Friday?'

'Right-ho.'

I couldn't wait to check out the list at school but by Friday only six genuine names had appeared and I wished two of those weren't there. Shelby was all right but Spencer Mason and Troy Hallett, both Year Sixes, thought they were 'it'.

School Football Team

Sign below:

Curtis Lamb

Alfie Cruickshank

Danny Ogle

David Beckham

Emile Heskey

Michael Owen

Shelby Newton

Troy Hallett (the best)

Spencer Mason (king)

Homer Simpson

Al COHOLIC

'Is that the lot? Six poxy names?' I said. Alfie pointed out that *was* nearly half the juniors. 'And no parent's volunteered to take us yet,' I moaned.

'Don't be down-hearted, chaps. Football practice at my house tonight, Shelby's coming too,' Alfie reminded us.

Well, it was *something* I supposed.

9

'This is your garden?' I gawped. Curtis and Shelby laughed. They'd both been here before.

'Told you it was adequate,' Alfie said. His lawn was so huge you could hardly see Westhorpe Hall, the massive house where Alfie lived, at the other end.

'You must be loaded,' I said.

'Of course,' Alfie replied matter-of-factly. 'Now can we get on with the football? I want you to teach me how to kick properly. I thought we could use Justin and Justout as goalposts.' He pointed to two naked stone cherubs a few metres apart.

'You're the boss.'

For half an hour Curtis and I took it in turns to show Alfie how to use different parts of his foot to pass and kick accurately. He *sort of* got the hang of it but kept trying to kick the ball as soon as it came to him without taming it first. Shelby, who had an older sister who played at secondary, was quite skilled. She had a strong left foot but got flustered if the ball didn't go exactly where she wanted it. 'I'm fed up of this. I'll go in goal,' she said.

'May I take a penalty like they do on TV?' Alfie begged.

'Sure,' we said, and stood back.

He rolled up his sleeves, licked his lips, ran, and kicked. Whack! The ball went straight into Justout's chubby belly and bounced off again into the distance.  'You've knocked his tinky-winky off!' Shelby shrieked.

'Help me look for it,' Alfie called, but we were too busy killing ourselves laughing.

None of us noticed the kid until he stepped out from behind the bushes. 'Do you want this?' he asked, holding the football.

'No, we want this,' Alfie grinned, holding up the stone willy. 'Who are you?'

 The kid shrugged. He was about our age, with long straggly hair dotted with coloured beads. 'I'm Devlin. My da's up at the house, asking if we can camp in your wood for a while.'

'Oh, OK,' Alfie said. He turned to us. 'Mother won't mind, she never does.'

'Can I join yous?' Devlin asked.

'Certainly,' Alfie agreed. 'You and I'll take Curtis and Danny. Shelby, are you OK in goal still?' Shelby nodded.

It was much better with five of us. I started off with possession and crossed it to Curtis, then ran forward. Alfie tried to tackle Curtis but he was too slow and Curtis dodged him easily, crossing back to me. Suddenly, Devlin arrived out of nowhere, trapped the ball deftly with his right, positioned himself, then shot forward with his left and fired. Shelby stood no chance. Nobody would have.

A shiver ran down my back. I'd seen enough magic players to know Devlin was one. 'Will you be going to school while you're here?' I asked. Devlin pulled a sour face and nodded.

'Seven!' we chorused.

'Same time, same place Monday?' Alfie suggested.

10

Devlin arrived late on Monday morning, looking uncomfortable. Spencer hissed in a low voice: 'Nose pegs, everybody, the gyppos have landed.'

I told him to bog off and made room for Devlin next to me.

At break, he signed up for the team. 'Can we still go ahead with only seven?' we asked Mrs Bulinski in the playground.

'We'll see,' she said. We all know what that means in teacher-speak. Desperate, I put up my own notice next to hers:

FOOTBALL IS THE *BEST* GAME IN THE WORLD

IT KEEPS YOU FIT

AND YOU MAKE NEW FRIENDS

Sign up now for the best time of your life

Please Please Please

Danny Ogle

At least I was playing *some* football, though. We met at Alfie's again and played in pairs with one of us taking it in turns in goal. Devlin was so good we soon learned that if we wanted a sniff of the ball we had to be on his side.

'Who coached you?' I asked when we stopped for a break.

'Nobody.'

'Well then, we can tell Mrs B we want nobody to coach us, too. That'll solve a problem!' Alfie joked, then groaned.

'What?' Curtis asked.

'Troy and Spencer,' Shelby sighed, nodding in the distance.

The two Year Sixes approached, swaggering. They were both wearing flashy replica kits of London Premiership teams. Troy had 'keepers gloves on. 'We thought we'd better turn up for practice seeing you *forgot* to invite us,' he said.

I hoped Alfie would tell them where to go but he just shrugged. 'I suppose we should play as a team,' he said.

'I'm in goal,' Troy declared, taking over.

'Shelby is in goal,' I pointed out.

'*Was* in goal, Yorkshire Pudding, *was* in

goal.' He strolled over and stood between Justin and Justout.

OK, Mason, I thought, let's see what you're made of. 'Alfie was just going to take a penalty,' I said.

'Was I?' Alfie asked.

'Yeah,' I reminded him, 'just like the one you took yesterday.'

His eyes lit up. 'Oh, yes, of course I was.'

'Aim for Justin,' I whispered, knowing he'd miss.

He rolled up his sleeves, licked his lips, ran, and kicked. Whack! Troy went down like a ton of bricks, rolling about and clutching his rude bits in his posh gloves. We all let out a sympathetic 'ooh!'

'I'll go back in goal for a while, shall I?' Shelby suggested.

'OK,' Troy squeaked.

They were all right after that, especially when they realized we might be younger but we were just as good. Neither of them played with much style but they were solid enough. Devlin, of course, was brilliant. 'Not bad for a gyppo,' Spencer admitted at the end. I could tell from the thunderous look on Devlin's face the name-calling wouldn't be lasting much longer and I pitied Spencer and Troy the day they pushed him too far.

But it was a start and I went home happy.

11

The trouble was, having a kick about with just seven of us lost its appeal after a while. Alfie's garden was big but it was still a garden which meant we spent half the time searching for the ball in the rhododendrons and half the time covering Justin and Justout's jangly-danglies with cycle helmets. It was mucking-about-in-the-park stuff. We had to work on Mrs Bulinski—quick.

The next time it was her break duty, Curtis, Alfie, and me followed her round the playground, pleading for a proper practice schedule after school, even though we only had seven people, not the ten she had stipulated.

Mrs Bulinski pushed her glasses up the bridge of her nose and sighed hard. 'All right,' she said, 'if it's so important to you, you can stay behind on Wednesdays and I'll ask someone else to do Gardening Club.'

Alfie immediately grabbed her hand and shook it. 'You really do set a magnificent example to the teaching profession, Mrs Bulinski. You should have a shopping centre named after you,' he stated, just a bit over the top. I mean, a statue would do.

Mrs Bulinski patted him on the shoulder. 'Thank you, Alfie, that's a very nice thought. Now, which one of you is going to break the news to Mr Spanner? He should be at home now if you want to pop round.'

There were groans from the other two. Alfie sounded as if his appendix had just burst. 'Can't you do it, miss?' Curtis said pitifully.

'No.'

'I can't go; I'm too young to die,' Alfie moaned.

'Blimey,' I said, heading for the gate, 'I'll go on my own. It's no wonder we haven't won the World Cup since 1966 with this attitude!'

'He was a good friend, that Danny Ogle,' Alfie sniffed sadly.

12

I only knew Mr Spanner by sight but he had a
fierce reputation. He didn't talk, he barked, and
then only one word at a time, such as 'litter!' or
'gate!' Even Hallett and Mason obeyed him
immediately, which is more than they did for
Mrs Bulinski sometimes.

I wasn't scared of him though. It had
nothing to do with being new and not
knowing any better. I had an advantage.
Confidently, I knocked on his door and
delivered the news.

Ten minutes later I was back in class. 'He's
alive! Praise the Lord!' Alfie shouted.

'What happened?' Curtis asked.

'We start tomorrow, 3.30 sharp.'

'You're joking! Didn't he go on about his
precious vegetables?'

'They did "crop up" during negotiations,' I
said wittily.

'And we're still allowed on?'

''Course,' I shrugged.

'How did you manage that?'

'I speak fluent caretaker-ish,' I said mysteriously.

Mum laughed when I told her about what I'd done. 'Aww, love. Didn't you tell them about your grandad?'

'I did afterwards.'

'Forty-six years as a school caretaker. He'd seen it all.'

Grandad died when I was seven but I remembered enough about him to handle Mr Spanner. Nasty weather on the field and nasty surprises down the bogs were the two things grandad hated most about the job. All I had to say to Mr Spanner was that I knew, I understood, I sympathized. I wouldn't say I won him over totally, but we each knew where we were coming from. I even wrote a list, with Mum's help, for his approval which I handed to him before the pitch inspection the next day.

TERMS AND AGREEMENTS

The team:

◎ No team member will trail back into school in muddy boots.

◎ No team member will trespass anywhere near the vegetable patches and flower beds.

◎ If a ball strays into one of the patches, it will be retrieved only with permission.

◎ We will look after all our equipment ourselves.

◎ We will not lose the key to the shed door or be forever asking where it is.

Mr Spanner:

◎ Will keep the football pitch in immaculate condition.

◎ Will arrange for lines to be painted before important matches.

◎ Will stop stray dogs from pooping on the pitch.

◎ Will put his clematis somewhere else.

Signed:

   D. Ogle **for the team**

Mr Spanner furrowed his thick grey eyebrows and went 'Hmph'. Which in caretaker-ish means 'agreed'. He then made us follow him round the edges of the field. We marched after him, in single file, as he pointed out areas we had to avoid on pain of death.

Eventually, Mrs Bulinski bustled across so we could start and Mr Spanner returned to school to begin his bin-emptying and toilet flushing. 'Right, are we set?' Mrs B asked.

We were in-deedy.

'And I see you've got all your equipment ready; that's excellent.'

I guess with not being sporty she would class four plastic cones and my leather ball from home as 'equipment' but never mind. She appeared to have brought her own equipment, too; a huge pile of paperwork, her mobile phone, and her chair. As she plonked herself down and opened a buff folder with the words 'numeracy and literacy policies' typed across it, I realized Mrs Bulinski had no intention of even pretending to coach us, she was just there to cover herself in case of accidents. Oh well.

I led us into the centre of the pitch. 'Shall I show you some of the warm-ups and drills we used to do at my old school?' I suggested. We hadn't really bothered at Alfie's but I knew how important they were. Trouble was, I couldn't convince anyone else. They ran round the pitch a couple of times and copied my muscle stretches but when I mentioned cone work they all looked at me blankly and said 'nah!'

'We just want to get on with it,' Troy said, sliding on his 'keeper's gloves and heading for the goalposts. It so annoyed me the way he thought he had a divine right to go in goal just because he had gloves. He wasn't even that good unless the ball came straight at him. Make him stretch either way and he was beaten every time, the plank.

45

Shelby was much better; she played a lot of basketball at home with her older sister and did karate so she was used to leaping about in all directions but she wouldn't say anything to Troy. The two Year Sixes thought they ruled.

It went OK, though. The ground was a bit bumpy in places but safe enough. It was good to get that feeling of a regular shaped playing area, even though we were only using half the pitch. Alfie's kicks were still the wildest and most unpredictable—an opposition's dream. Only Devlin's speed saved the dahlias from instant splattering time and time again. 'It's not fair! I aim one way and it goes the other. It looks so easy on TV!' Alfie grumbled, getting more and more flustered and upset. 'Why can't I do it?'

Poor Alfie.

Then something strange happened. Mr Spanner, who must have finished his bin emptying and toilet flushing in the fastest

time ever, suddenly reappeared. He stood by the wing and scowled. That wasn't the strange bit. The strange bit was that for the last twenty minutes of practice hardly one of Alfie's shots went out of touch. Every time the ball looked in danger of escaping Mr Spanner would bellow: 'carrots! carrots!' or 'kale! kale!' and look so fierce that Alfie somehow managed to bring the ball under control and whack it desperately away to safety. We made him man of the match.

'Is that it?' Mrs Bulinski asked, looking up in surprise as we trudged past her.

'That's it,' I told her. 'Unless you'll let us stay on longer,' I added hopefully.

'Not today, I'm afraid, Danny, not today.'

I knew from her expression she hadn't watched any of the match but I tried not to mind. She had given up her time to be with us, which is more than anyone else had.

13

Shelby brought her best friend, Alyce Laverack, the following week. 'I'm fed up of being the only girl so I've made her come,' Shelby explained, before adding in a loud whisper, 'Plus she fancies you.'

'I do not!' Alyce protested, going red and elbowing Shelby in the ribs.

'Three times round the field,' I sighed, leading the jog. Great. That was all I needed— love stuff. She'd better not mess about being all girlie or she could get lost.

I think Shelby's teasing had annoyed her, though, because Alyce didn't mess about at all. At first, she seemed really nervous, not even attempting to go for the ball but after we tapped it to her a few times, she got stuck in. Mr Spanner only shouted 'cabbages! cabbages!' at her once which caught her off-guard but she soon got used to the bellowing. She was quite nippy, too, though nothing like Devlin. Devlin was the star but Alyce Laverack would do.

'You were good,' I said to her. 'Will you come next week?'

'If you want me to.'

'Ooooh! "If you want me to!"' Troy mocked as he passed.

'Where are you going?' I said, ignoring his comment.

'What's it to do with you? We've finished, haven't we, *sir*.'

'It's yours and Spencer's turn to put the equipment away,' I pointed out.

'Like that's going to happen!' he said, unstrapping his keeper's gloves before spitting hard into the grass. He and Spencer spent a lot of time spitting—I reckon they think it makes them look professional.

'We're only talking about a few lousy cones,' I pointed out.

'Exactly,' he sneered and walked off with his sidekick.

14

It was Monday lunchtime. Devlin and I had to sit on Troy and Spencer's table, worse luck. Spencer began dishing out the shepherd's pie. Somehow he always ended up as server at dinner times, just as Troy always ended up as goalie during practices.

'Is that enough for you, Devlin?' Spencer asked in a dead clever voice as he served Devlin's portion. 'We know how hungry you must be, living in a *caravan*.' He also knew as well as everyone else that Devlin was a vegetarian and had a special meal made for him.

Devlin pushed his plate away. 'I don't eat meat,' he said testily.

'Go hungry, then,' Troy retorted, sliding the plate to a Year Two girl across from him.

Devlin was a weird kid. He could have

smacked either of them with one arm tied behind his back but he never did, no matter what they said to him. I knew Devlin would just have sat there, starving, if nobody did anything, so I put my hand up. 'Yes, Danny?' the dinner assistant, Mrs Howells, asked.

'Have you got Devlin's dinner, miss?'

'Of course I've got his dinner. One of the servers should have collected it.' She fetched the separate meal and placed it in front of Devlin, telling Spencer and Troy off for not doing their job properly.

They homed in on me straight away.

'See your lot got thrashed again,' Troy mocked. Town had gone down two–one on Saturday. Not that I'd been allowed to listen to the highlights on the radio. Oh no. I'd had to go round three poxy houses which were for sale on The Lawns. And we couldn't have morning appointments, could we? Oh no. We could only be fitted in between three and five. Estate agents were obviously not into football. They weren't into finding us anywhere decent either. Every house had been awful—all modern and

no character. Mum had got stressed because time was running out on the cottage and Karla had started crying, saying she liked the cottage and why couldn't we buy that and Steve had snapped at her so I'd shouted, 'Don't yell at her, you're not our dad.' We all ended up walking back to Low Street in silence. Mum had forced me to listen to one of those long, embarrassing chats about Steve not wanting to replace my dad and all that kind of stuff. I hated those—they made me squirm, even though I knew she was right. Finally I'd gone upstairs to phone Gran for a match report only to find we'd been disallowed a penalty in the eighty-ninth minute. All-in-all I was not in the mood for one of Hallett's get-at-the-new-kid sessions.

'We're fifth in the league,' I pointed out to him.

'Yeah, for how long?'

Spencer added his two-pennyworth. 'I don't know why you bother supporting a lame team like that, anyway.'

I could feel my face glowing. Nobody supported Town at Westhorpe—it wasn't local enough and it wasn't one of the glory teams that kids like guess-who followed, either. 'Well, I bet you've never even been to London to see yours play,' I retorted.

Troy splattered baked beans next to my pie. 'Who needs to? They're always on TV because they're the best.'

'You should be supporting your local side like City or County,' I persisted.

'We will when they're top of the Premiership.'

'Fickle,' I said angrily. Glory supporters really did my head in.

'What did you call us?' Spencer asked, shoving his face dangerously close to mine. I could feel the atmosphere around our table change as everyone waited for my reaction.

I backed off. I didn't want to start something I couldn't finish. 'Nothing,' I mumbled, feeling irritated at myself for giving in so easily.

15

Mrs Bulinski told us during registration she wanted to see the football team at break.

'I bet you anything she's cancelling training on Wednesday,' Curtis whispered. 'She'll have a meeting or something.'

I felt my heart sink but Mrs Bulinski seemed too pleased with herself for that. She had a huge grin on her face when she addressed us. 'Well, you'll never guess what I've done?' she said, dipping a chocolate bourbon into her coffee cup.

'Signed up for Arsenal?' Troy suggested.

Mrs B continued smoothly. 'Be sensible, Troy. How can I play for Arsenal and run a school at the same time? I'd never get my marking done, would I? No, this is a bit more realistic.'

'What? Tell us, miss,' Shelby asked.

'I have got you a match next week!'

A match? Much as I wanted to play against another team I knew we were nowhere near ready.

'Who against, miss?' Curtis asked.

'Tuxton,' she said blithely.

'But they'll slaughter us!' Curtis protested.

Mrs Bulinski shook her head. 'No they won't. You see, I bumped into Mr Girton last Friday at a headteachers' meeting and told him all about you and how we're just starting out and he's arranged to have his 'C' team play you. Seven-a-side after school next Wednesday. They'll come here.'

A 'C' team? How did a school not much bigger than ours manage to get a 'C' team?

'Well,' she said, looking a bit crestfallen by our silence, 'aren't you pleased? Curtis? Danny? It's what you wanted, isn't it?'

'I guess so but . . .'

'Good!' she said. 'I'll let you go and tell Mr Spanner, then.'

16

I managed to persuade Mr Spanner to let us practise on the field at lunchtimes leading up to the fixture. He agreed but turned up to 'tend' his plots like I knew he would. Everybody moaned when they saw him but secretly I was glad. We played better with the names of vegetables ringing in our ears. If only Mr Spanner showed as much interest in football as he did potatoes, we'd have been sorted but he told me he was a cricket man himself and that football was blown all out of proportion these days. Ah well.

I woke up on Wednesday morning with that familiar match-day tingle in my stomach. Sometimes it became so bad before a game, I thought I might throw up but today was just a tingle.

'Make sure you have a big lunch,' Mum advised.

Steve said he'd try and get there, Karla lent me her lucky coin, and Gran sent me a quick e-mail.

> Go get 'em, Danny.
> Let me know what happens.
>
> PS: Green's injured—hamstring.

I arrived earlier than usual at school to ask Mrs Bulinski to put a team list on the notice board. She seemed distracted and pointed to a heap of papers on her desk. 'I've got to sort out these job applications this morning, Danny, can't you do it?'

OK, I admit when I'd started all this the idea of being captain was appealing but this was managerial stuff. 'It's easier if you do,' I replied, knowing what Troy and Spencer would say if I selected the team I wanted. Unfortunately, I hadn't caught Mrs B at a good time.

'Go on, Danny. You're the experienced one,'

she said with just the tiniest hint of irritation in her voice.

But I wasn't the experienced one! Give a kid a break, missus. I tried again. 'If I write the names down will you copy it out?'

There was a curt nod of the head which I took as a 'yes'. Quickly, I scribbled down my list.

Westhorpe Primary School

Fixture list

Westhorpe v Tuxton 'C' team

3.45 pm Wednesday October 11th

Shelby Newton (goal)

Troy Hallett

Spencer Mason

Devlin Black

Curtis Lamb (captain)

Danny Ogle

Alfie Cruickshank

Sub: Alyce Laverack

Support welcome but mind the vegtables

Guess what happened? My scribbled list appeared in all its glory on the notice board with a pencil line through 'vegetables' because I'd spelt it wrong. 'I just haven't had time to copy it out,' Mrs Bulinski said with a hint of irritation in her voice that wasn't quite so tiny this time.

At lunch, more crossings out had appeared. This time, someone had scribbled out 'goal' next to Shelby's name and put it next to Troy's and somehow Spencer was now the captain.

'What are you going to do about it?' Curtis asked.

What was *I* going to do about it? After the episode at dinner time last Monday I didn't want any more confrontations with those two doofers. 'Nothing!' I replied coolly. 'What are *you* going to do?'

'See Mrs Bulinski.'

'Good luck, mate'

And Mrs B's reply to Curtis? 'Well, does it really matter who's the captain? I'm sure you can sort it out between you.' Can you imagine the England manager doing that? No, me neither.

* * *

At three forty, we paraded on to the pitch, dressed in our feeble games kits, under the feeble leadership of Spencer flipping-feeble Mason.

We stood and watched as a new minibus pulled up at the side of the road. A tall man with a bald head and long nose like Postman Pat's emerged—presumably Mr Girton—followed by his team. They walked briskly after him in single file, all kitted out in dark green strips with yellow and green hooped socks. Very smart.

'They're a bit little, aren't they?' I asked. Hardly any of them looked more than seven or eight years old, apart from two at the back.

'That's Adam and Ellie,' Curtis cried out, waving to them, 'the Huckerby twins, remember, we told you they'd moved to do more sport.'

'They don't look very happy about it,' I said, glancing at their long faces.

'They're not. Ellie told me she hates school now.'

I shrugged. It was not my problem.

Mr Girton was refereeing, with Mrs Bulinski and Mr Spanner both watching from the touchline. Alyce and the twins stood nearby, chatting. 'Ten minutes each way,' Girton declared briskly, blowing his whistle to start.

With that sound, I forgot everything. I just wanted to play.

I intercepted their first pass from the kick-off and crossed the ball to Curtis. Curtis ran halfway up the field, swerving round a defender and crossed to Devlin who just had to tap it in. The goalie, a curly-haired kid with freckles, looked lost against our full-sized goalposts and

didn't have a clue which way to dive. One–nil in ten seconds. Dream start!

Mrs Bulinski clapped politely and Mr Spanner frowned as the lad trampled across his potatoes to retrieve the ball. The goal gave us the boost we needed and we were away. I held mid-field, feeding and assisting with Shelby alongside. Spencer stayed back in defence and Alfie just ran anywhere his little legs could carry him. By half time it was five–one to us, with Devlin scoring four and Curtis the fifth.

I should have been happy but I wasn't. It was too easy. The Tuxton team were trying but we were just older and bigger and stronger. Spencer was the worst; he just barged into anyone approaching the goal, sending them flying with his rough tackles, despite being cautioned a

couple of times by an increasingly angry Mr Girton. 'This is so easy,' he bragged, exchanging a hi-five with Troy at half time.

Mr Girton obviously thought so too. He subbed his two defenders for Adam and Ellie, muttering furiously into each twin's ear as he did so.

'I might as well use our sub, too,' Spencer said and indicated for Alyce to get ready. 'You're off, Ogle,' he shouted.

Big surprise.

Strange as it sounds, I wasn't that bothered. This match was turning into a joke as far as I was concerned.

It looked worse from the touchline. Even with the twins, Tuxton couldn't make much impact on the game. Devlin was just in a class of his own. Part of me willed him to have the ball all the time so that I could enjoy his performance, part of me felt sorry for the opposition. I think Devlin did, too. By his eighth goal he had begun apologizing to the goalie and started fetching the ball for him. The poor kid was nearly in tears.

'We seem to be doing very well,' Mrs Bulinski whispered to me.

'Yeah,' I replied, 'just a bit.'

Girton blew the whistle a minute early. 'What do you say, team?' he barked. 'Three cheers to Westhorpe. Hip hip . . .'

Spencer, as captain, should have returned the gesture but was too busy punching the air in victory. Fortunately we had Alfie, who went up to each dejected player and shook their hand in turn before going back into school to get changed with the others. I hung around, planning to help Mr Spanner with any damaged plants—a deal's a deal.

I overheard Girton refuse Mrs Bulinski's invitation to come back into school for refreshments. 'No time, sorry,' he said, a tight smile on his lips.

'Well, thank you for coming,' Mrs Bulinski began.

'Huh! Well, you certainly had me fooled, Laura,' he snapped.

'Pardon?' she asked, her face going slightly pink at Girton's tone.

'Not played before? Just starting out? Do you think I would have turned up with that shambolic lot if I'd known you had a ringer?'

Mr Girton's face was turning a nasty red. I'd seen it before; that dark, threatening colour on faces of managers who couldn't bear losing, on parents' faces, screaming from the touchline if their kids made a mistake.

'A ringer?' Mrs Bulinski asked.

Mr Girton almost spat. 'A ringer—a pro. The lad who needs a haircut!'

'Oh, you mean Devlin.'

'Whatever his name is. Whose books is he on?'

'Er . . .' Mrs Bulinski hesitated, puzzled by the question, 'he's fond of animal stories—*Lucy Daniels* and . . .'

'Not those sort of books! Never mind. I want a return match next week. At Tuxton, on a proper seven-a-side pitch. Four o'clock sharp.'

'Well . . . of course . . . Terry . . . that'll be all right, won't it, Danny?' Mrs Bulinski asked, catching sight of me.

'I'm not sure, miss,' I began.

Girton cut me dead. 'That's fine, then, four o'clock. Twenty minutes each way.'

With that, he stormed off.

'I've never seen him like that before,' Mrs Bulinski said.

'I'll bet he's never lost eleven—three before,' I replied.

17

I had a bad feeling about next week's match which nobody seemed to take seriously.

'We'll just be more even,' Curtis said. 'It'll be a better game. Chill out, Danny.'

'You don't have to play if you don't want to, Ogle,' Spencer quipped. 'We scored more goals in the second half without you.'

I didn't let him get to me because I knew he didn't have a clue. He still hadn't cottoned on that for one person to score the goal (e.g. Devlin) another had to make the goal (e.g. me) and not just welly the ball into outer space and hope for the best (e.g. him).

Only Grandma shared my concerns. 'What do you reckon?' I asked her when I called her at the weekend. 'Hmm. Girton's not gracious in defeat by the sound of it. He'll be coming out

69

with all guns blazing, Danny, no doubt about it.'

'What can we do?'

'Take plenty of vitamins and pray.'

I did all I could to prepare us for the return match. I hunted out some old boots and shin pads for Alfie because he hadn't any. Shelby's sister donated the same to Devlin, but he refused. 'These are fine,' he said, pointing to his well-worn trainers. They had scored eight goals last week, so who could disagree?

We practised after school a few times. Troy and Spencer didn't bother to turn up—they had better things to do than 'panic like a pudding'.

After each practice we bought sweets and pop from Mrs Dobbs' shop. The day before the match, Ellie and Adam Huckerby came in just as we were going out. Shelby told them we'd hang on for them. 'Fraternizing with the enemy,' I teased as we plonked ourselves down on the bench outside.

'They're not the enemy. Just because they go

to a different school doesn't mean I can't talk to them, does it?'

'I suppose.'

'Right then,' she said, pinching a green Skittle and grinning.

When Ellie and Adam joined us, there was only one topic of conversation. 'Are you both in the team tomorrow?' Shelby asked.

Ellie laughed. 'Us? Not likely. We've never been picked before and we won't be again. He says we're beyond help.'

'Yeah—the only reason we played against you was because he thought it would be nice for us to show Mrs Bulinski what her ex-pupils could do,' Adam sniffed.

'Well, that plan went wrong,' Alfie smirked.

'Yeah, and didn't *we* know about it the next day,' Adam said miserably.

He exchanged looks with Ellie but didn't elaborate. 'Will you be watching though?' Curtis asked.

'Oh yes—we wouldn't miss it for the world,' Ellie said. She glanced around nervously. 'You'd better warn Spencer to be careful. That was Josh Gibbons's little brother he kept cropping last week. Josh is *so* going to get even.'

'Is he good?' I asked.

'He's in Forest's under-twelve squad.'

'Oh. *That* good.'

'He's not even the best player, though,' Adam added. 'There's Max Gaskin, Simon Machin, Joachim, Hannah . . .' He reeled off a load more names. What made it worse was you could tell he wasn't even bragging about it, just stating facts. My worries about the match multiplied faster than bugs in mouldy fish.

'Well, we've got Dev,' Alfie said proudly. 'Nobody can be better than Dev.'

The twins stared at Devlin admiringly. 'You were brilliant,' Ellie said, 'but . . .'

'But what?' Shelby asked.

'But Mr Girton says one player doesn't make a team and the rest of you are a bunch of talentless, untrained no-hopers who run around like headless chickens and wouldn't know the code of conduct if it slapped you in the face.'

'No offence,' Adam added.

There was a long pause as everybody took in Mr Girton's little speech.

Devlin grunted something. 'What?' I prompted, hoping for some words of inspiration from our star.

'I saw a headless chicken once,' he said quietly.

'Did you? Was it disgusting?' Alfie asked.

Devlin nodded. 'Why do you think I don't eat meat?' he muttered.

As words of inspiration go, they weren't the best I'd heard.

18

I couldn't eat a thing the morning of the match and it had nothing to do with Devlin's chicken. I was almost in a trance as Mum opened the post. 'More rubbish,' she frowned.

'What is it?' Karla asked.

'From the estate agents—they know we can't afford houses at these prices but they send the details anyway,' she complained, screwing up the envelope. I went to stand by the door, hoping she would be too distracted to nag me about breakfast. No chance. 'You need something in your stomach to give you energy, Danny,' she said.

I already had something in my stomach. A massive lead weight. 'I'm not hungry,' I complained.

She threw me a banana and said 'sit'.

The day dragged. Literacy Hour felt like Literacy Month. Maths, lunchtime, science, and music all merged into one long pain in the neck. The lead weight in my stomach got heavier and heavier until, finally, the bell went and it was time.

Mrs Bulinski was taking half of us to Tuxton in her car, Mrs Newton the other half in hers. I clambered in the back of Mrs Newton's car with Devlin and Alyce.

'Don't talk to us, Mum, we've got to get psyched up,' Shelby ordered from the front seat.

'Will this help, petal?' Mrs Newton replied, turning the radio higher. It was playing 'We will rock you' but it didn't help at all.

There was quite a crowd gathered as we arrived at Tuxton School. Ellie and Adam were there, plus several of the little kids from the 'C' team, as well as a stack of parents. They stared at us with a mild curiosity as we made our way towards Mrs Bulinski and the other half of our team. I guess we'd caused a bit of a stir last week and they wanted to see what we looked like.

'Well, they haven't even got a proper kit,' one of the adults whispered loudly as we passed.

'That's him—that's the good one,' I heard Ellie say to a man—maybe her dad—as Devlin went by. A murmur arose as word got round the crowd and everyone craned their necks to see him.

I felt a sudden stab of envy. Nobody had ever said that about me. I glanced at Devlin but his eyes were on the pitch and I knew the admiration had washed right over him. He was silent and edgy; all he wanted to do was get on with the game. We had that much in common, at least.

Girton came up to us and read us the riot act. 'Right, Westhorpe,' he snapped, 'as I seem to be refereeing again I just want to make a few things clear to you before we start. First off, I will not accept any back-chat, cheating, or foul play, is that clear?'

We all nodded but it was Spencer and Troy he was staring at. I saw Spencer whisper something to Troy out of the side of his mouth. 'Second,' Girton continued, 'as this is a seven-a-side match you will be playing on a correctly set-up seven-a-side pitch with appropriately sized goalmouth.' He pointed to the goalposts, which were half the size of the ones at Westhorpe and had proper nets attached. 'There will be no offside rule, of course, but free kicks and penalties will be given if necessary. As this is a friendly, you can play as many subs as you like . . .'

'We've only got one,' I said, pointing to Alyce.

'Really? What a shame,' he replied drily.

I glanced across at the pitch—there were at least twelve Tuxton kids out there. 'Can we bring the same people on and off, then, sir?' I wanted to know.

'I don't see why not,' he agreed. I think the

'sir' had taken him by surprise. He seemed to thaw a bit. 'You the captain?'

'No, I am,' Spencer said, barging forward. Mr Girton looked unimpressed. 'Better get your team into position then.'

'Never thought of that,' Spencer muttered but luckily Girton didn't hear.

'It should be easier to score with those smaller goals, shouldn't it?' Alfie asked as we walked on to the pitch.

'We'll know soon enough,' I said. I stared wistfully as the Tuxton lot huddled in a circle, arms round each other, doing a motivational chant. We used to do those. It really puts the willies up the other team.

'How do you want us to play?' I asked our captain, just on the off-chance he had a plan.

He looked baffled, 'What do you mean "how?" Like normal, that's how.'

We were doomed, then.

19

You know after a match on telly when managers are being interviewed and they come out with classic stuff like, 'If the ball had gone in it would have been a goal'?

Well: if Devlin hadn't been so tightly marked, we could have passed to him, then he'd have scored . . .

If Spencer hadn't been such a fouler he wouldn't have given away so many free kicks and penalties, they wouldn't have scored (so often) . . .

If Alfie had stopped standing there with his mouth open and tried to get just one tackle in . . .

If Mrs Newton hadn't put Shelby off by shouting 'Go get 'em, sweetheart!' at the top of her voice . . .

If Troy had been less of a plank . . .

Score at half time?

Seven–nil.

We had a five minute gap before the next innings.

Spencer gave us his opinion of what was wrong with the game. 'They're a right bunch of cheats,' he muttered. 'They're only winning cos it's a home match. Talk about a dodgy referee. Not one of those was a penalty–not one!'

'Yeah,' Troy agreed.

'And what's happened to you, wonder boy?' Spencer hissed as Devlin took a swig of water.

'What do you mean?' Devlin asked.

'You're playing rubbish. Get some goals in or else!'

'How can we score goals if nobody passes the ball to us?' Curtis yelled. We started arguing like mad until Alyce noticed Adam Huckerby approaching. 'Shh!' she said, 'don't let him think we're ruffled.'

We stood back and pretended we liked being thrashed. 'Nice pitch they've got, isn't it?' Shelby said, trying to keep her voice level.

'Yeah; ball's good quality too,' I added.

'And this lemon squash is jolly decent,' Alfie boomed, holding up his plastic cup against the light.

Adam wasn't fooled one bit. 'How's it feel to be losing?' he asked.

'Bog off, if you've just come to rub it in,' Troy warned.

The boy lowered his voice. 'I'm not. I've just come to wish you luck.'

'Why?'

'The good players are coming on next.'

'What?' Spencer cried.

'Oh, yeah,' Adam said, dead serious. 'That was just the B team. Josh Gibbons is warming up now—he's nicknamed you DMW.'

Spencer frowned. 'DMW? What does that mean?'

'It's the name they give to prisoners on death row in America before they're executed. It means Dead Man Walking.'

We turned in silence to where the Tuxton team stood. A tall kid with a spiky haircut looked across and met our gaze. Coolly, he

looked away, said something to another team mate and laughed.

'Right,' Spencer said, bending down and pulling out his shin pads.

'What you doing?' Troy asked.

'Subbing myself off. Alyce can take over in defence. I'm not staying on there to be done in.'

'Come on,' I said, 'you'll be all right. It's not fair to put Alyce . . .'

He came down on me like a ton of bricks. 'Shurrup, Ogle. If you think you can do any better, you take over!'

'He can and he will!' a familiar voice cut in.

I spun round in surprise. 'Gran!' I shouted. 'What are you doing here?'

'Don't you lot ever read your e-mails?' she grinned.

20

With Gran's arrival there was a buzz about the team. In that one minute of rest time remaining, she gave us all such fantastic advice we completely turned the match around. Tuxton didn't know what had hit them. Within seconds of the second half, Devlin scored. I followed up with a hat-trick . . .

Yeah, you're right. That *does* only happen in books, and stupid books at that.

We got thumped.

Well and truly thumped.

Tuxton had scored twice before Troy had had time to do his first spit. Plus they were making substitutions every few minutes, bringing on fresh legs. Not because they needed to—just to show they could.

Having Gran there did make a difference to

me, though. It gave me the courage to do some decision making. Well, *someone* had to. Just before Tuxton were about to take a throw-in, I motioned to Girton to hang fire. I made Troy swap with Shelby. Troy hesitated for a second, glancing across for instructions from his mate. Waste of time. Spencer wasn't there—he'd disappeared. Wordlessly, Troy handed over his gloves to Shelby and took up her position at the back.

Things improved a little. Shelby pulled off a few good saves and brought their success rate down from one hundred per cent to about fifty per cent on target. I won the ball in mid field a couple of times and tried to pass to Devlin but

 they still had him under wraps. 'Use Curtis! Use Curtis!' Gran shouted. I did, more and more, during our rare moments of possession. Curtis managed to get a

couple of good shots in but hit the keeper's legs both times. The narrower nets meant you needed greater accuracy.

About five minutes from time, I had possession but only Alfie was in any decent space. I lobbed the ball to him but he froze and I knew he was just going to welly it any old how off the pitch and it would be their throw-in yet again. I darted forward to receive the ball back screaming 'cabbages! cabbages!' and he stopped, grinned and played it neatly back to me.

For once, Devlin had escaped and he sprang across to my right. 'Man on!' Gran shouted, but I'd already crossed it to Dev. He dribbled between two players, dummied a third and

shot from just inside the halfway line. Bang! Straight into the back of the net.

It was the best goal of the match. Tuxton were rattled then, and Devlin scored another two in quick succession but Girton blew the whistle and it was all over.

Readers who don't want to know the final score, look away now.

(It was 13–3 to them!)

21

Gran gave me a proud hug. 'Well played,' she said.

'Er, Gran, we were hammered.'

'It's only your second match as a team, what do you expect? You did your best, that's what counts.'

'Try telling them that,' I said as we watched the rest of the team shuffle miserably towards the car park.

'Oh, they'll live,' Gran said unsympathetically, 'a good team always bounces back. I told you about that time Town lost ten–one to Man. City, didn't I?'

'Once or twice,' I said, almost managing a smile.

'And look where they ended up a couple of years ago—ha! No, Danny, there's always another match, always another season. You've got the makings of a good team there, if you cut out the rubbish.'

'Do you mean Alfie?' I asked quietly.

'What, the little lad running round in circles? No, I don't! At least he tried. I mean that little slack-jack over there!' She pointed to Spencer who was mouthing furiously to Mrs Bulinski about something. 'I can't stand that sort of bad attitude. He wants to shape up!'

'We all do,' I sighed as I walked with her to her car.

'The best thing you can do is get out there and have another match. Now give us a kiss and tell your mum I'll see her soon.'

I leaned close and kissed the side without the mole and waved goodbye.

She's ace, my Gran.

22

Mum and Steve were full of concern. 'Wow! That's more like a rugby result than a football one,' Mum said.

'No need to rub it in, Mum.'

'Never mind, Danny,' Steve smiled, 'we've got something to tell you that might cheer you up.'

'Oh, yeah?' I asked.

He slid a folder across to me. 'Your mum and I have just looked round this place. It's called Chestnut House and the good news is, it's in Tuxton.'

'Tuxton?' Karla said grumpily.

'Yes, land of the mighty footballing school!' Steve grinned.

'What about me? I like it here. I want to stay here! I've just settled!' Karla sulked, stalking off.

Mum and Steve exchanged helpless looks.

'I'll go,' Mum sighed, following Karla upstairs.

'What do you think?' Steve asked, pointing to a photograph of a semi-detached house with a huge chestnut tree in the front of it.

'I don't know,' I replied.

'It's got a superb lawned garden and it's only a five minute walk to the school,' he continued eagerly.

I stared at the photograph. The house looked fine—much better than anything we had seen so far. 'We've made an appointment to look round at the weekend,' Steve stated, 'and it's empty—we could move in straight away.'

I didn't sleep much that night. I had these two voices in my head, arguing with each other. 'Well, you have to be out of the cottage in a few weeks anyway, so siding with Karla won't do any good,' one voice said. 'And the house is in Tuxton. You could be playing alongside Josh Gibbons and all those other kids. You could have Girton as a teacher—just think of those lovely, long games lessons!'

'Yeah, but Tuxton doesn't have Curtis and Alfie and Devlin,' the other voice said. 'And

Mrs Bulinski is kind and teaches well, even if she isn't big on sport.'

'So what?' sneered the first voice. 'Football is all that matters.'

I woke up confused. What I needed was a sign.

23

And there it was, greeting me first thing when I arrived at school.

> There will be no more football practices until further notice.
>
> *Mrs Bulinski*

'What's that all about?' Curtis groaned.

'Don't ask me,' I said.

'Let's ask her.'

'We can't, she's discussing the teachers' interviews with Mummy and the other governors,' Alfie informed us.

Spencer solved the mystery. 'My dad's done that,' he smirked.

'What do you mean?' I asked.

'He phoned Mrs Bulinski up at home last night and gave her a right ear-bashing about us playing a top team when we weren't ready. My dad told her she could get sued for putting us through such a traumatic experience. I bet that's why she's stopped the practices.'

I couldn't believe what I was hearing. 'Well, that's just what we need, isn't it? Fewer practices are bound to make us better players. That makes sense!' I burst out.

'Keep your hair on,' Spencer replied coolly. 'She won't do anything, she never does.'

'Exactly! That's the whole point! It takes her all her time just to turn up and now she's not even going to that! Nobody else will do it so we're finished, aren't we? No more Westhorpe Primary School Football Team!'

Spencer just shrugged as if to say 'so what?' Trust him to ruin everything. I could feel the anger bubbling up inside me like hot fat in a chip pan. I knew this time I wouldn't back off. 'You've really messed up,' I said fiercely, wanting him to make just one crack—just one.

Then Alfie let me down. 'Maybe it's for the

best,' he sighed, 'maybe we should just go back to playing in my garden again and forget being a team. We were slightly pathetic yesterday.'

Then Curtis let me down. 'Yeah, and at least we won't have Spanner staring at us all the time at Alfie's.'

Then Alyce let me down. 'And I'd like to see Justout's famous missing tinky-winky,' she grinned.

The best bit was, they were being serious. I thought of Chestnut House, empty and waiting in Tuxton. 'Fine!' I cried, throwing my hands up in despair, 'go back to Alfie's if that's what you want but you can count me out. I want to play proper football with a proper team, not a bunch of losers who give up the first time something lousy happens to them.'

They stared at me in stunned silence. Then Spencer finally stuck his oar in. 'Tch! Listen to him! He's not even that good—all he does is run round shouting orders at people—any nerd can do that!'

That did it.

Mason was toast.

I clenched my fist, ready to punch his lights out but bloomin' Devlin held me back. I struggled but he had a strong grip. 'He's not worth it, Dan,' he hissed in my ear, 'his type never are. They start it but you're the one who gets done, especially when you're new. Let it go.'

'Gerroff, Devlin!' I yelled, still too angry to listen to common sense.

'Devlin's right,' Troy added. *Troy* added?

I blinked at the older kid. 'What?'

Troy stared calmly back. 'He's right. Spencer's not worth it.'

'What are you trying to say?' Spencer asked his mate, a confused look on his face.

His mate squared up to him. 'At least Danny

stayed on the field yesterday. He's got more guts than you have!'

'How has he?' Spencer blustered.

Hallett glared fiercely back. 'You dropped us all in it, Spenny. Whatever happens you don't let your school down like that. My dad killed himself laughing when I told him the score but he got mad when I told him what you'd done. He said that was yellow. You weren't Dead Man Walking yesterday—you were Dead Man Poohing!'

'Say that again,' Spencer snarled.

Troy repeated the accusation, spacing the words out deliberately slowly. 'Dead Man Poohing!'

 'That does it, maggot breath!' Spencer screamed and let fly.

It was a great scrap.

Pity Mrs Speed stopped it halfway through.

* * *

'Blimey,' Curtis said, scratching the back of his neck, 'I've never seen them fall out before.'

'Did you see that punch? Troy ought to take up boxing!' Shelby added.

Alfie was still gazing after the troublemakers. 'I hadn't thought of it like that before,' he said, frowning.

'What?' I asked.

'What Mr Hallett said about letting the school down. We did a bit, didn't we?'

I shrugged, 'They were a stronger side—we were always going to lose.'

'I suppose,' Alfie agreed, 'but we didn't need to lose so heavily, did we? If we'd listened to you more about drills and things.'

Finally!

'Yeah, and they already knew about Devlin —other teams don't,' Shelby continued excitedly, 'which means we stand a better chance next time we play a game.'

'Yes, oh yes, of course! Because if Tuxton are the best, other teams aren't the best!' Alfie cried.

Curtis turned to me. 'You didn't mean it, did you, about playing for another side, Danny? You're one of us, right?'

I looked at the ground and didn't answer.

24

We were all called in to Mrs Bulinski's office to give our side of the story. I'd never seen Mrs Bulinski so cross. Jets of spit flew out of her mouth as she rounded on us during our explanation. 'This just sums up that silly game totally as far as I'm concerned!' she bellowed, glowering furiously at Spencer and Troy who were standing, heads down, next to the photocopier. 'Fighting! Over football! Of all the idiotic things!'

She paced up and down a few times before scribbling her signature at the foot of a letter. I glanced briefly at it , saw it was for Mr and Mrs Hallett, then waited until she slotted the letter into an envelope. 'Aren't there going to be *any* more practices after school, miss?' I asked nervously. She didn't know just how important her answer was.

Mrs Bulinski glanced coldly at me. 'Can you give me one good reason why there should be, Danny? Because I can't think of one. In the space of two weeks I've been accused of . . . of match-fixing, I've been accused of destroying a child's self-esteem . . .' Her eyes drilled such a hole in to Spencer's back I thought he'd split in half. I opened my mouth to speak but she'd really got ants in her pants. 'And now this! Fighting—and in front of the governors—as if I hadn't enough on my plate with interviews tomorrow. Competitive games just bring out the worst in people and this just proves it,' she fired. I opened my mouth to protest but the woman wasn't even stopping for breath. 'I've always felt so,' she railed. 'Oh, it's fine for those few who have talent but what about those who haven't? Those who are picked last every time there's a Games lesson because nobody wants them on their team? Being made to feel like a reject because you're too fat or too slow or too clumsy? It doesn't count that you're good at playing the clarinet or have the singing voice of an angel. Oh no, it's how well you can kick a ball that counts in this day and age. Well, not in my school it isn't! I always vowed no pupil of mine would go through what I had to—'

She stopped abruptly and blinked, then added limply, 'Anyway, I miss Gardening Club.'

25

It didn't take a genius to work out who the slow, fat, clumsy kid was. It was crystal clear now why Mrs Bulinski hated Games. Still, did it matter? By Christmas I could be one of Girton's lads, playing all the soccer I'd dreamed of, wearing a smart kit, practising with proper equipment—the lot. I had wanted a sign and here it was but . . . but deep down, it wasn't the one I wanted. I glanced round the room.

Apart from Troy and Spencer, I liked everyone here, even Mrs B, if she'd calm down a bit. And I mean really liked—like best mates standard liked. OK, Spencer and Troy were pains in the butt at times but there had been bigger pains with bigger butts at my old school, too. And who was to say Tuxton kids would be any better—in fact, *could* they be any better? Who could make me laugh more than Alfie or impress me more than Devlin? They thought of me as one of them—Curtis had just said so, hadn't he? I couldn't let them down. I made my decision there and then. I'd play football like I supported football—not for the glory team but for the team where my heart was. I would stay at Westhorpe. All I had to do now was convince Mrs B to change her mind about practices.

'Miss,' I said quietly, 'I know what you must think about football but you're only getting one side of the picture. It's like whenever there's any trouble at an international, the cameras only show the idiots having street fights.'

'Letting their country down!' she exclaimed bitterly.

'But it's only a few that mess it up for the rest of us. The cameras never show you the thousands of normal fans just singing and cheering their team on. In fact, if you came to where I sit in the Town ground, you'd think you were in a library, it's that quiet sometimes.'

She gave me a brief, polite smile but then glanced at her watch so I hurried on desperately.

I thought of all the PSE lessons and assemblies she loved taking. 'And playing football here has helped me to settle in to school. I've made new friends quickly and that's important. My mum thinks so too; she says she'd recommend the school to anyone.' I was rewarded with a nod. 'And football's good for equal opportunities,' I said, 'it doesn't matter what colour you are or whether you're a girl or a boy or rich or poor . . .' A double nod. I was definitely on the right track now. 'Football helps family life, too,' I garbled. 'When Dad phones up from Germany, the first thing we talk about is how Town are doing. If we didn't have that we'd have those dead long pauses because we've nothing else to say—I haven't even seen him since Grandad's funeral when I was seven.'

I stopped to swallow. I never talked about my dad in front of people. Still, it was out now so I might as well carry on with the personal stuff. 'And when Grandad died, it brought me much closer to my gran. We kind of lost touch when Mum and Dad divorced and Mum started going out with Steve, especially with Dad being so far away in Germany. He's Gran's son, you see, my dad.' I thought I'd better add that bit in case she was getting confused. Everybody else seemed to be, judging by the looks  on their faces. I carried on regardless. 'We all met up again at Grandad's funeral. Gran gave me Grandad's Town bobble hat and scarf and said it seemed a shame to waste the old goat's season ticket too, so I started going with her to matches and we got back to being a family again.'

Everybody in the office let out a quiet 'ahh'. 'Gran says without football she'd be a lonely old lady mumbling to herself in the bus station,' I ended sorrowfully.

That last bit was a right fib but I could have sworn I saw a tear in Mrs Bulinski's eye and I thought I'd won her over but we were interrupted by the phone ringing. The moment was lost and we were shooed out.

26

I felt really dumb as we trooped back to Mrs Speed's lesson but Shelby gave me a friendly punch and Alfie said it was the best speech he had ever heard in his life. It was Spencer who surprised me the most, though. At lunch-time break Mrs Howells asked me to fetch the milk for the infants. As I dashed round the back of the school I almost tripped over his foot. I had forgotten he had to stand outside this entrance, Troy at the other, as part of their punishment for fighting.

'Sorry,' he muttered as he pulled his foot back.

I made for the door but Mason put his hand out and grabbed my sweatshirt. I swung round, ready to deck him if he started, but he let go instantly. 'I thought it was good—all that stuff you said to Mrs Bulinski,' he said. He sounded serious enough.

'Yeah, well . . .'

'I'm gonna get my dad to phone her, you know, and tell her he didn't mean it about suing.'

I was tempted to say something like: *'Pity he said it in the first place, dingbat,'* but something about his manner stopped me. He reminded me of that football I'd found in the shed that day—battered and deflated.

Mason kicked a small pebble across the tarmacked path, looked briefly at me then away again. 'He's like me is my dad . . . he gets mad quick . . . then afterwards he wishes he hadn't said half the things he said . . .'

'Yeah, well.'

'And you know what you were saying about your gran and grandad and that?'

I nodded.

'My dad hasn't spoken to my nan for years and we're not allowed to talk to her even though she only lives on the farm across from us. I never even get a birthday card. Nothing. Don't tell anyone, though.'

'I won't.'

'And you know all that Yorkshire Pudding stuff I come out with—I don't mean it, it's just a joke.'

'Jokes are meant to make you laugh,' I said.

'Yeah,' he agreed sorrowfully, 'I know, I'll ease off.'

Blinking heck—he'd be hugging me in a minute! I tried to think of something friendly in return. 'Your eye looks swell,' I laughed.

Gingerly, Spencer touched the puffy eyelid. 'Troy always could thump hard,' he said, flinching slightly.

'Mates, eh?' I mumbled. There was a pause. I remembered the milk and began to walk off but Mason held me back again, less roughly

this time. 'It's been good since you came,' he said unexpectedly.

'What do you mean?'

'Getting the team going. We all wanted to play football but we could never be bothered to push for it. Since you came we've had matches and everything. You've done great. And telling her everything just then . . . that takes guts.'

I stared at him, waiting for the punchline but instead he just glanced away, looking uncomfortable. 'I'll never let the team down again, I promise,' he said.

I waited for a second but couldn't hear or see any sign of a thunderbolt zapping towards him so maybe he meant it.

That night, I informed Steve and Mum I wanted to stay in Westhorpe, even if Mrs Bulinski refused to run practices. They looked dumbstruck. 'But what about playing decent football?' Mum asked.

'What can I say? I like a challenge,' I replied.

She sighed hard. 'Talk about unpredictable.'

27

Of course, I was Karla's favourite brother again. 'Cool! We can live here now and I can have my bedroom decorated properly. I'm having purple walls, stars and stripes curtains, and one of those cabin beds that you climb up with a ladder and come down by slide and you're not going on it.'

'Yeah, right,' I said, 'and I'm having mine done out in blue and I want a hammock all the way across the ceiling but there's just one small problem—this isn't our house. We've got to leave at the end of December remember, when the owners come back from Dubai.'

She shook her head vigorously. 'They're not coming back! The man's got to stay another two years so he says he might as well sell the cottage and we can buy it.'

'Since when?'

'Since last week but Mum and Steve didn't want to say anything because they were trying to find you somewhere else because of your stupid football! Favourite!'

'As if!'

'As if not!'

'I can prove I'm not their favourite,' I said.

'How?'

'Like this!' I picked up one of the cushions from the back of the sofa and belted her over the head with it.

She let out a massive roar and swiftly took up her weapon, the other cushion, and lunged. The battle had begun. It didn't take long for Mum to come charging in. 'Now what?' she

blared, calming down when she saw we were only messing about.

'We're just doing our homework!' I lied unconvincingly.

'What is it? Drama?' Mum fired.

'No, we've got to think of three questions to ask the new teachers,' Karla said, managing to drop her cushion behind the table before picking up her notepad.

'Yeah,' I said, admiring her for her quick thinking. 'Three questions.'

'I'm being serious,' Karla laughed, showing me what she had written.

1. Are you strict?
2. What is your favourite colour?
3. What is your favourite book?

By Karla Maria Ogle aged 8

'I'm looking for a sometimes, bright orange, and *Matilda* as my perfect combination,' she informed us.

'And what are you going to ask, Danny boy?' Mum teased, hands on hips. I scribbled something quickly.

'Show me,' Karla said, snatching at the pad. She shook her head and sighed.

---

1. Do you like football?
2. What football team do you support?
3. Will you be willing to train our football team after school?

Danny O.

'You are so sad,' she said.

After supper the four of us had a long chat about how things had changed since we'd moved to the countryside. Steve said he had a lot more work because there wasn't as much competition as in the towns. He'd already got bookings for weddings all through the following summer. Mum said she felt less stressed knowing she didn't have to worry about us getting squashed by a juggernaut every time we went out on our bikes. Karla said she liked walking to school on her own instead of having to go in the car.

'What about you, Danny?' Mum prompted. 'What has been the biggest change for you?'

'Apart from going to a new school, making loads of new friends, being an hour and a half away from the Town ground instead of ten minutes, and playing football for a side who went down thirteen–three you mean?'

'Yes, apart from that.'

'Nothing much.'

28

Now that I was definitely staying at Westhorpe, I took the interviewing process a little more seriously. Well, I was a country boy now; these things mattered. We don't have the luxury of dozens of teachers all in one school like townies. If we get a bad one we're stuck with them right from Year Three to Year Six. Think about it!

So when Mrs Bulinski introduced us to the four candidates the next morning, I scrutinized them thoroughly.

Candidate one fell at the first hurdle as far as I was concerned. 'I don't like football, I'm afraid,' she said, 'I think it's over-rated.'

Not as over-rated as your haircut, I thought.

Candidate two wasn't much better. 'I don't mind when it's the World Cup or something but otherwise I prefer rugby.'

Rugby? They couldn't even get the ball the right shape.

Candidate three was the bloke, a Mr Pearson. 'Yes, I like football,' he said. I felt my hopes rise. On to question two. 'Which football team do you support?'

'Manchester United.'

'Why?'

'That wasn't your third question,' Karla pounced.

'Why?' I repeated. 'Are you from Manchester?'

'No, I'm from Bristol. It's just that I've always supported them.'

'Will you train our football team if you are selected today?' I asked.

'Sure, if I've got time,' he agreed.

Hm. Apart from his choice of team, the guy had possibilities.

Candidate four was a Miss Craig. Her answer to my first question? She loved football. Her answer to my second question? Mansfield Town.

'I think you should always support your local team,' she explained when asked the reason for her choice.

Her answer to my third question? 'I'd love to.' *Love to!*

Well, it was all too obvious, wasn't it? 'The job's yours!' I told Miss Craig.

She smiled. 'Does that mean I don't have to meet the governors?'

29

The good news was, Miss Craig was offered the job and accepted it; the bad news was, she couldn't start until after Christmas. 'It's only eight weeks away,' Alfie pointed out.

'That's eight weeks without training,' I pointed out back.

'No, it isn't,' Alfie said smugly, 'look.'

He stood aside to reveal a new notice.

Westhorpe Football Team
Practices will begin after
October half-term.
Wednesday lunchtimes

Mrs Bulinski

Please note: practices will be
cancelled <u>immediately</u> if there
is any bad behaviour.

'Bless her little pop socks!' I grinned.

Practices were totally different this time. Nobody argued. Nobody complained about drills and set plays. We all just got on with it. Even Spencer. I think the fight with Troy had knocked some sense into him because he was way less mouthy. There were no more comments about gyppos and Yorkshire Puddings from either of them. It was all 'Over here, Danny' and 'Played, Dev.'

Even Mr Spanner seemed happy to let us practise without doling out the scowls and grunts. Once, when Alfie had managed to dribble the ball halfway down the pitch without tripping up, the caretaker actually clapped and muttered something amazingly close to, 'Well done, lad.'

'You know what's happening,' I said as we trooped off after our last practice before Christmas holidays.

'What?' Curtis asked.

'We're actually playing like a team.'

There were a few nods. 'Thanks to you, Oggy,' Curtis said, clapping me hard on the back.

'Yeah,' I agreed, 'I am pretty brilliant, aren't I?'

'Big head,' Alfie laughed and cupped his hands together half-singing, half-shrieking, 'There's only one Danny Ogle, one Danny Ogle, but he is an ugly kid!'

I was about to whack him when Shelby and Alyce fell into step next to me. 'Ask him,' Alyce nudged.

'No, you ask him,' Shelby replied.

I stared at them both and walked faster. There'd been a lot of sloppy stuff going on at end of term discos and parties lately. I began to get worried. 'What?' I snapped, thinking if one of them yanked a sprig of mistletoe above me it was better to get it over and done with quick.

'Do you think we could take on Tuxton again?' Shelby asked.

''Course we could,' I replied with relief.

'We'd still lose, though, right?'

'Let's have a think,' I replied. 'We don't have a coach yet, they do, we don't have any proper equipment, they do, we don't have a decent strip, they do. The answer is—probably,' I conceded, 'but the best thing about football is that it ain't over till the referee walks off with his guide dog.'

'A straight yes or no would have done,' Shelby grumbled.

'Well, I don't know, do I? Why, anyway?'

'Just curious,' she said, wiggling her eyebrows up and down. 'Ellie told me Mr Girton's arranging a massive seven-a-side tournament in March. He's inviting all the local schools.'

'And talent scouts from Lincoln and Nottingham will be there. It's going to be a biggie,' Alyce added.

'We'll be there too!' I said instantly, 'Watch out for Westhorpe!'

Shelby grinned. 'I thought you'd say that. Oh, and Danny?'

'What?'

She leaned forward and gave me a right smacker on the cheek. She didn't have any mistletoe, either. They've got a nerve, these village girls.